Wallace Hoskins
The Boy Who Grew Down

Iris

Wallace

Horace

by Cynthia Zarin

illustrations by Martin Matje

A DK INK BOOK
DK PUBLISHING, INC.

A Richard Jackson Book

DK Publishing, Inc.
95 Madison Avenue
New York, New York 10016

Visit us on the World Wide Web at http://www.dk.com

Library of Congress Cataloging-in-Publication Data
Zarin, Cynthia.
Wallace Hoskins, the boy who grew down / written by Cynthia Zarin; illustrated by Martin Matje.—1st ed.
p. cm.
"A DK Ink book."
Summary: Small for his age, Wallace always wears a fireman's hat so he won't be lost in a crowd,
but when his legs start growing out of proportion to his body,
his mother is told by old Nanny Heppleweather that the hat must come off.
ISBN 0-7894-2523-8
[1. Size—Fiction. 2. Growth—Fiction. 3. Family life—Fiction.]
I. Matje, Martin, ill. II. Title. PZ7.Z263Wa1 1999 [E]—DC21 97-52627 CIP AC

The illustrations were created with China ink and watercolor.
The text of this book is set in 16 point Janson Text.
Printed and bound in U.S.A.
First Edition, 1999
2   4   6   8   10   9   7   5   3   1

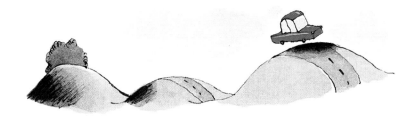

For the Zoodus
—C.Z.

For Ambroise, my lucky little godson
who never wears a fireman's hat
—M.M.

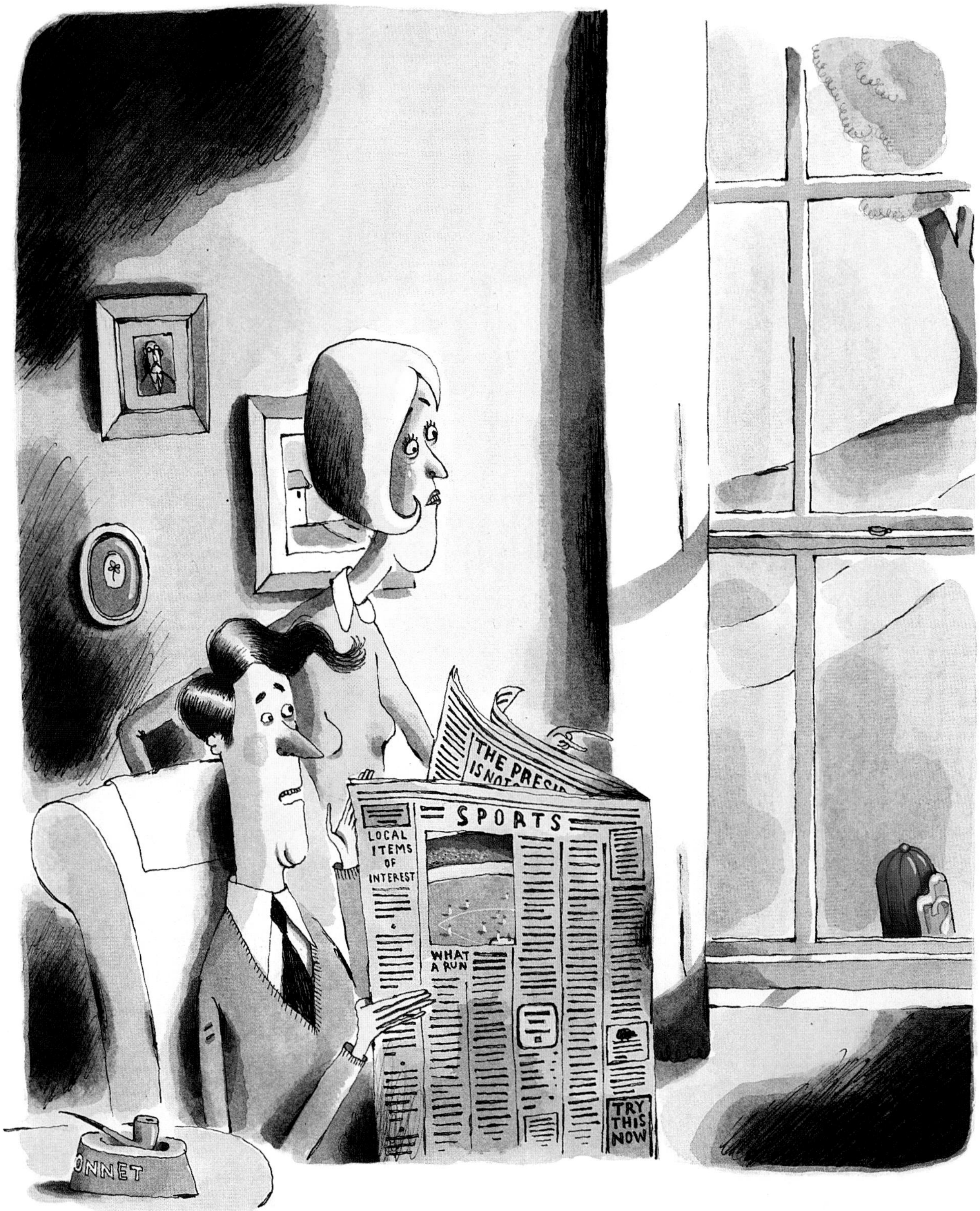
SPORTS
LOCAL ITEMS OF INTEREST
WHAT A RUN
TRY THIS NOW
ONNET

*O*nce there was a boy named Wallace Hoskins. In almost every respect, Wallace was an ordinary boy. He knew how to make a kite out of newspaper, and how to put two pieces of grass together to make a whistle. He had an older brother named Horace and a baby sister called Iris. Wallace liked to ride his bike. He also liked his red fireman's hat.

He wore it at meals and he wore it to school. He wore it in the bathtub and he wore it to bed. The hat had been a present from his uncle Cyrus on his fifth birthday, and Wallace was fond of it.

Sometimes Wallace's mother complained about the hat.

"I do wish, Fergus," she said to Wallace's father, "that he would take the hat off."

"Don't worry," said Wallace's father. "He'll grow out of it."

But that, you see, was the problem. Wallace was turning out to be a very small boy. When he ate his breakfast, his legs were too short for him to rest his feet on the chair rung. When a pair of shoes or blue jeans wore out, his mother bought him a new pair, in the same size. While he could go hand over hand on the monkey bars, he first had to ask someone to pick him up. If a balloon (even one with a very long string) floated up to the ceiling, Wallace had to get a step stool to bring it down.

Wallace was philosophical about his size. He hardly thought about it. Often, though, he tried to think up ways to do things on his own without asking for help. For Christmas, he asked for, and received, a pogo stick. If he woke up feeling he'd like to be taller, he put on his roller skates. Or he climbed a tree. Because he always wore his fireman's hat, he was never lost in a crowd.

Sometimes Wallace's mother worried about him.

"Don't fuss, Gladys," said Wallace's father. "He'll grow out of it."

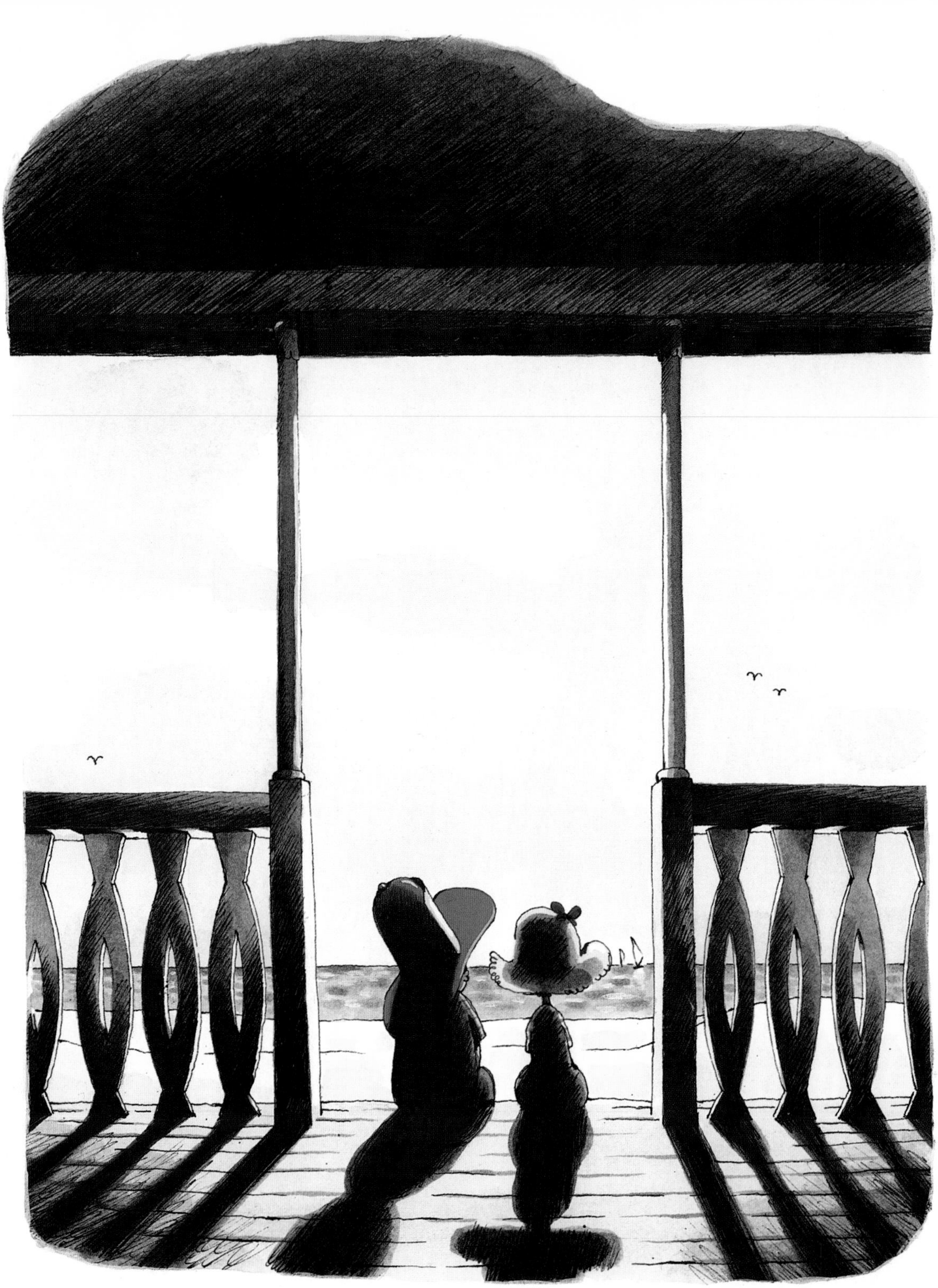

The years passed. The summer Wallace was eight and a half, the Hoskins family rented a cottage on a beach. From their front porch they could see far out into the bay. Gulls flew overhead. Sitting on the cottage steps, Wallace and Iris were exactly the same size, but when Iris stood up, she was taller.

Every day at the beach was blue, peaceful, and full of sunshine. One morning, however (it was a Tuesday), Wallace's mother made an astonishing discovery. When Wallace's father came into the kitchen he found her pointing, wordlessly but with a wild look in her eyes, at Wallace's feet.

"Fergus," said Wallace's mother, "look at his ankles!"

"They look perfectly ordinary to me," said Mr. Hoskins.

"It's his pants!" said Wallace's mother. "They fit him just two weeks ago! Our Wallace is growing!"

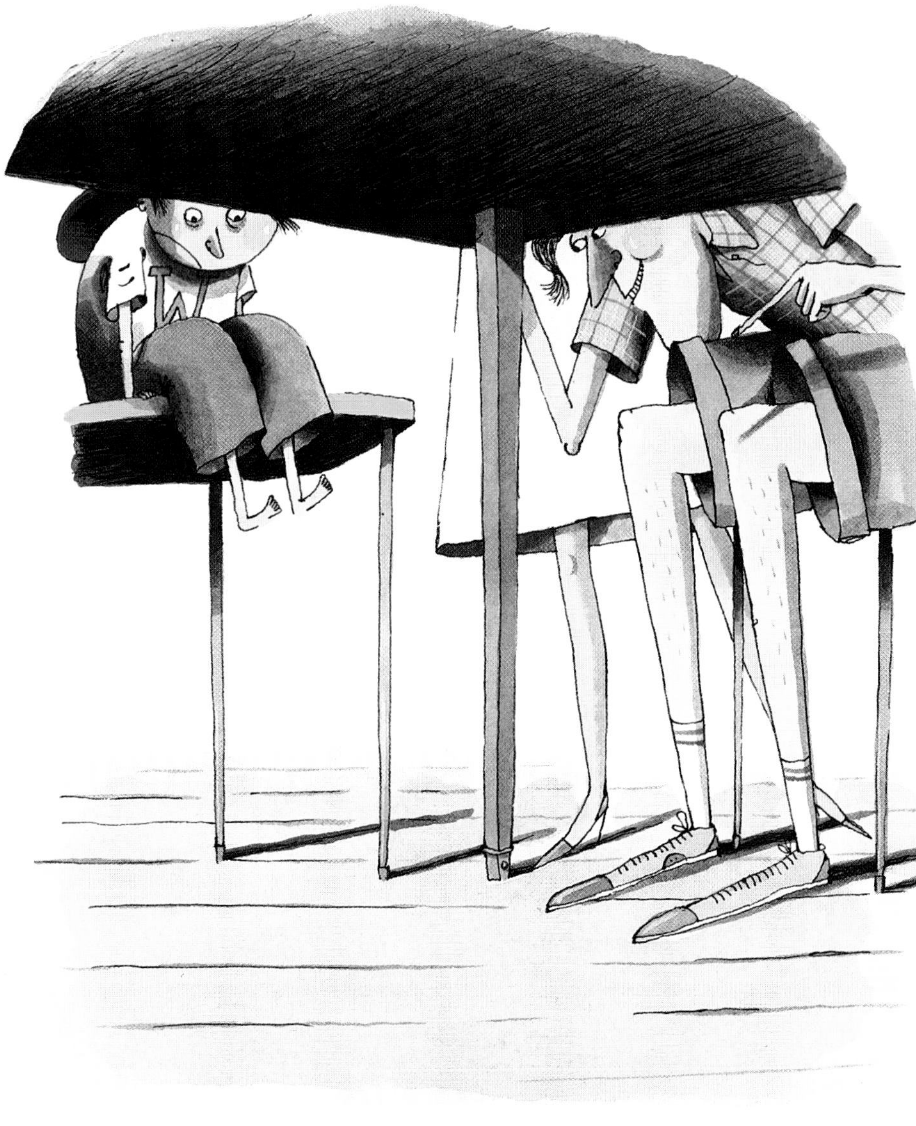
W

Mrs. Hoskins whipped a tape measure out of her sewing basket. She measured his height, his width, his arms, and his legs. She measured his head, what she could find of it under his hat.

"Wallace," she announced, "has grown two inches."

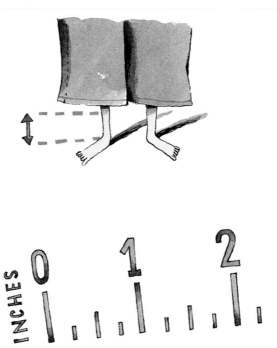

Dramatic as these events might seem, they made little difference to Wallace. He was used to being the size he was. But he was glad his mother was happy because he knew she worried about him.

Within the hour, Wallace's mother had driven to town and returned with a new pair of blue jeans for Wallace, and a new pair of sneakers.

"Hooray for Wallace," she said as he put them on.

"I didn't do anything," said Wallace, "but thank you just the same for the sneakers." They were red, and they matched his fireman's hat.

For Wallace, the next few days were halcyon. He and Iris swam in the high tide, and they looked for crabs when the tide was out. He found a starfish. His new sneakers got wet. But his jeans, although he forgot to roll them up, stayed dry.

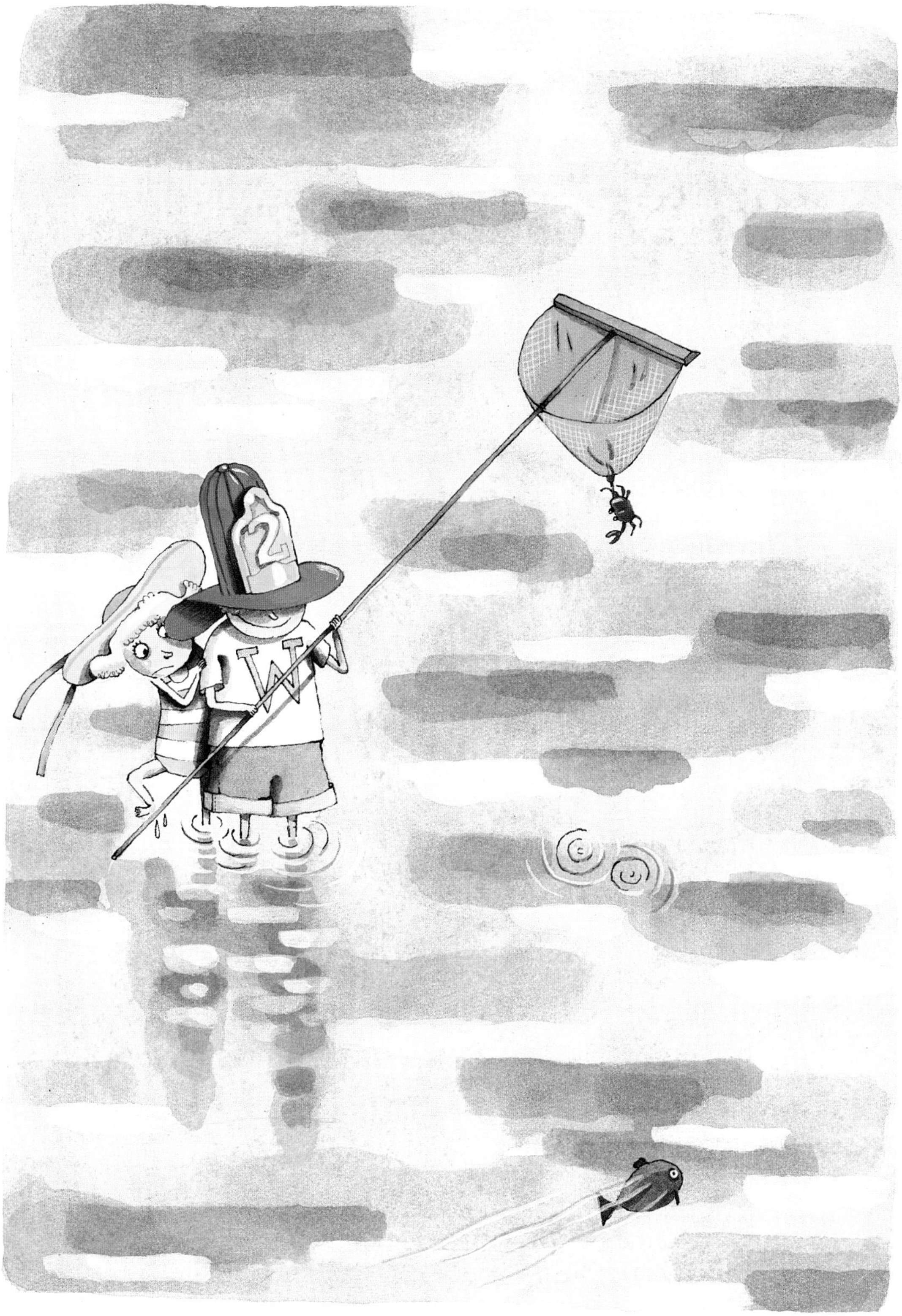

Years later, when he was older, Wallace looked back on these days fondly. Would he have acted differently if he had known about the events to come? For by that Saturday evening, it was clear—at least to Wallace—that something peculiar was happening to him.

HIS LEGS WERE GETTING LONGER, BUT THE REST OF HIM WAS STAYING THE SAME SIZE.

How could this be? What could be done about it? By inclination, Wallace disliked anything that called attention to himself. But he knew it was only a matter of time before someone else noticed his predicament. His brother Horace, who had a scientific bent of mind, had been eyeing him strangely since yesterday.

Up until now Wallace had been happy. Now he was worried. What if his legs never stopped growing? Underneath his fireman's hat Wallace's hair stood on end. He tried to look on the bright side. He thought about basketball and finding owls' nests in high branches. He thought about being able to disentangle kite strings from telephone wires. Perhaps I'll be able to talk to the stars, thought Wallace. Without shouting.

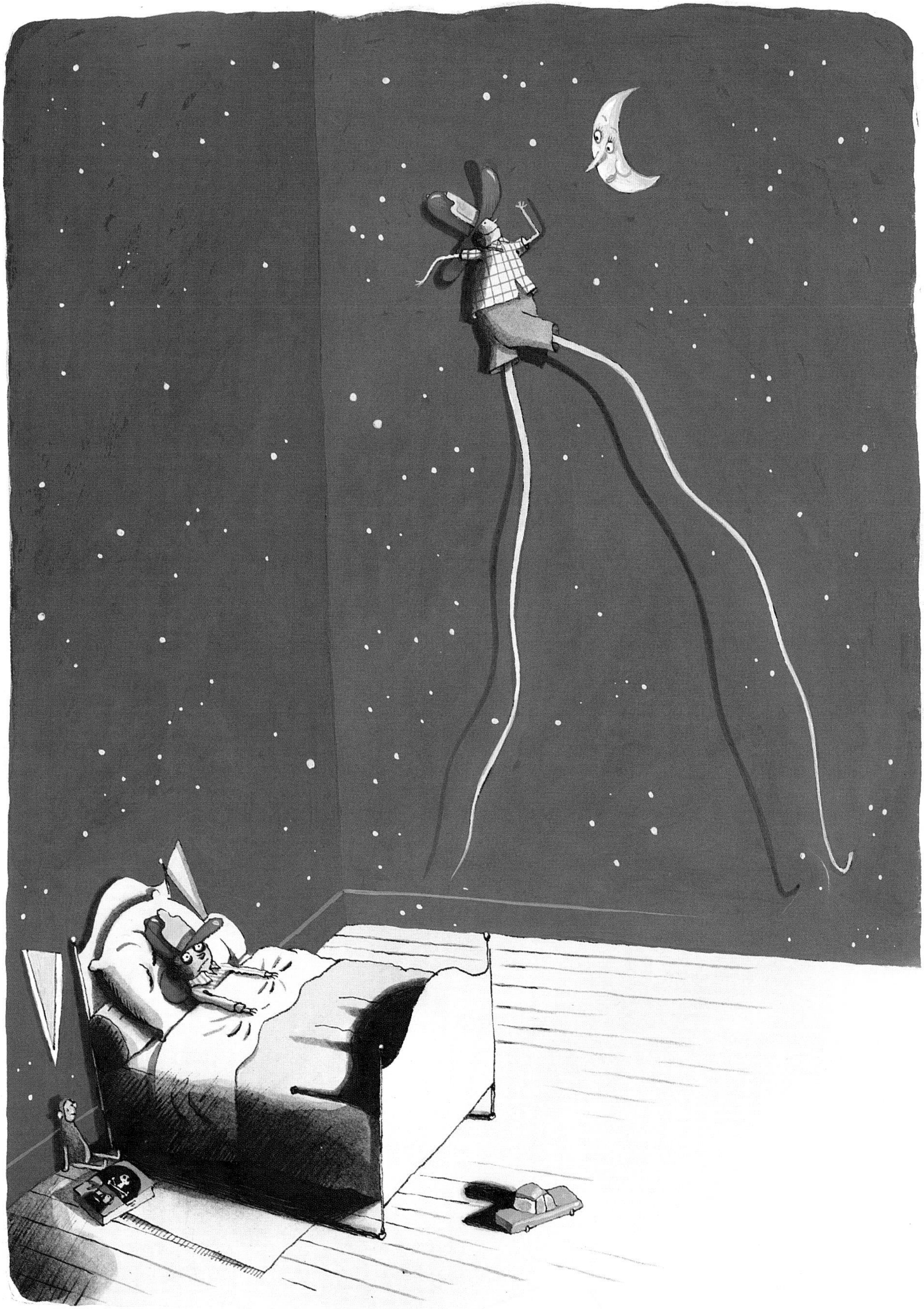

It was no use. Every moment his feet seemed to be growing farther away from him. It was depressing. He walked down to the beach. It was dusk, and the water was turning green and violet.

Meanwhile, Wallace had been right about Horace. Horace

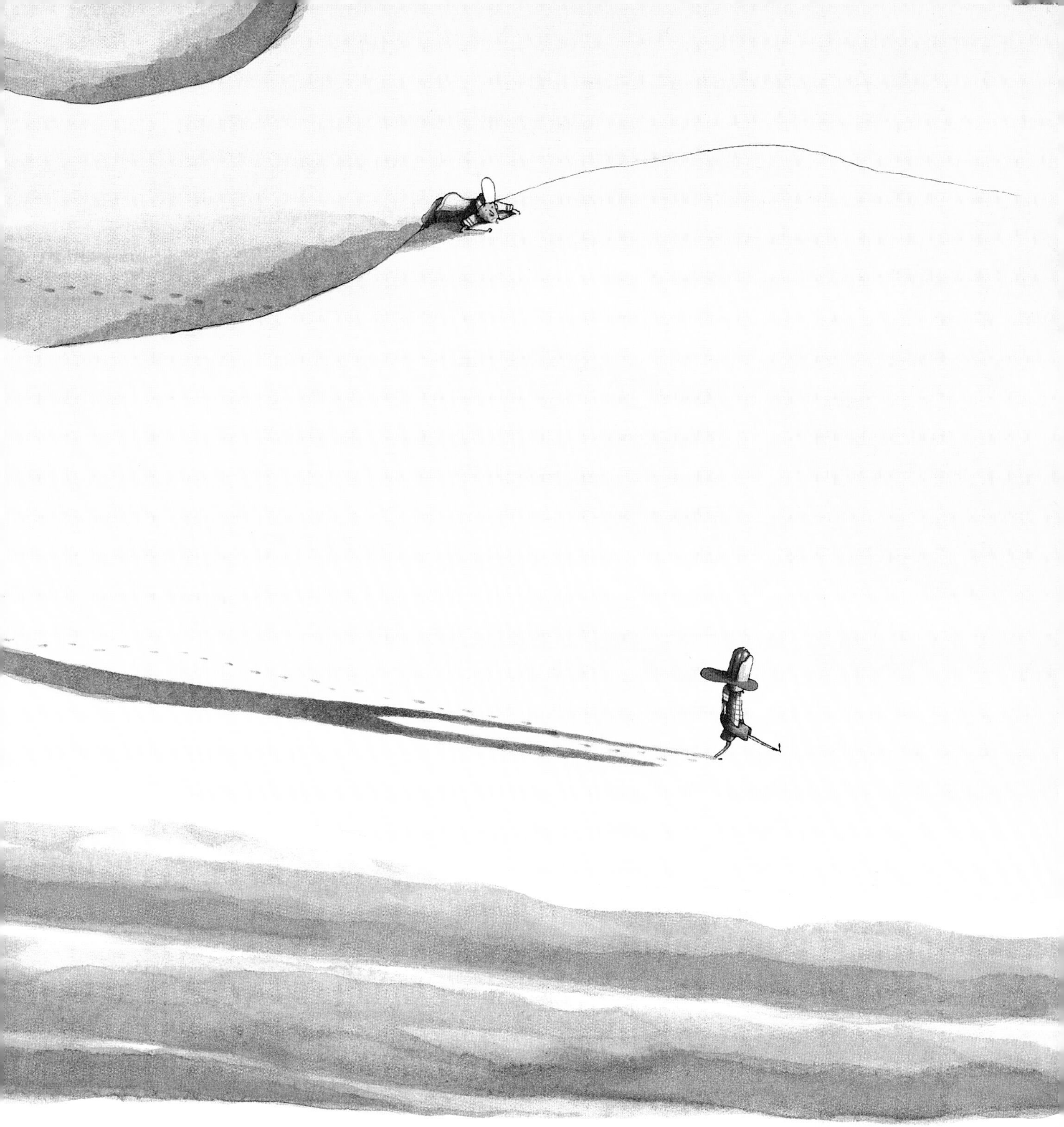

had noticed. In fact Horace had been doing very little else but keeping watch. When Wallace trudged up from the beach, Horace saw how long his shadow was against the dune, and how his legs stretched up like thin pipe cleaners from his faraway feet. Under his fireman's hat, Wallace's face looked quiet and sad.

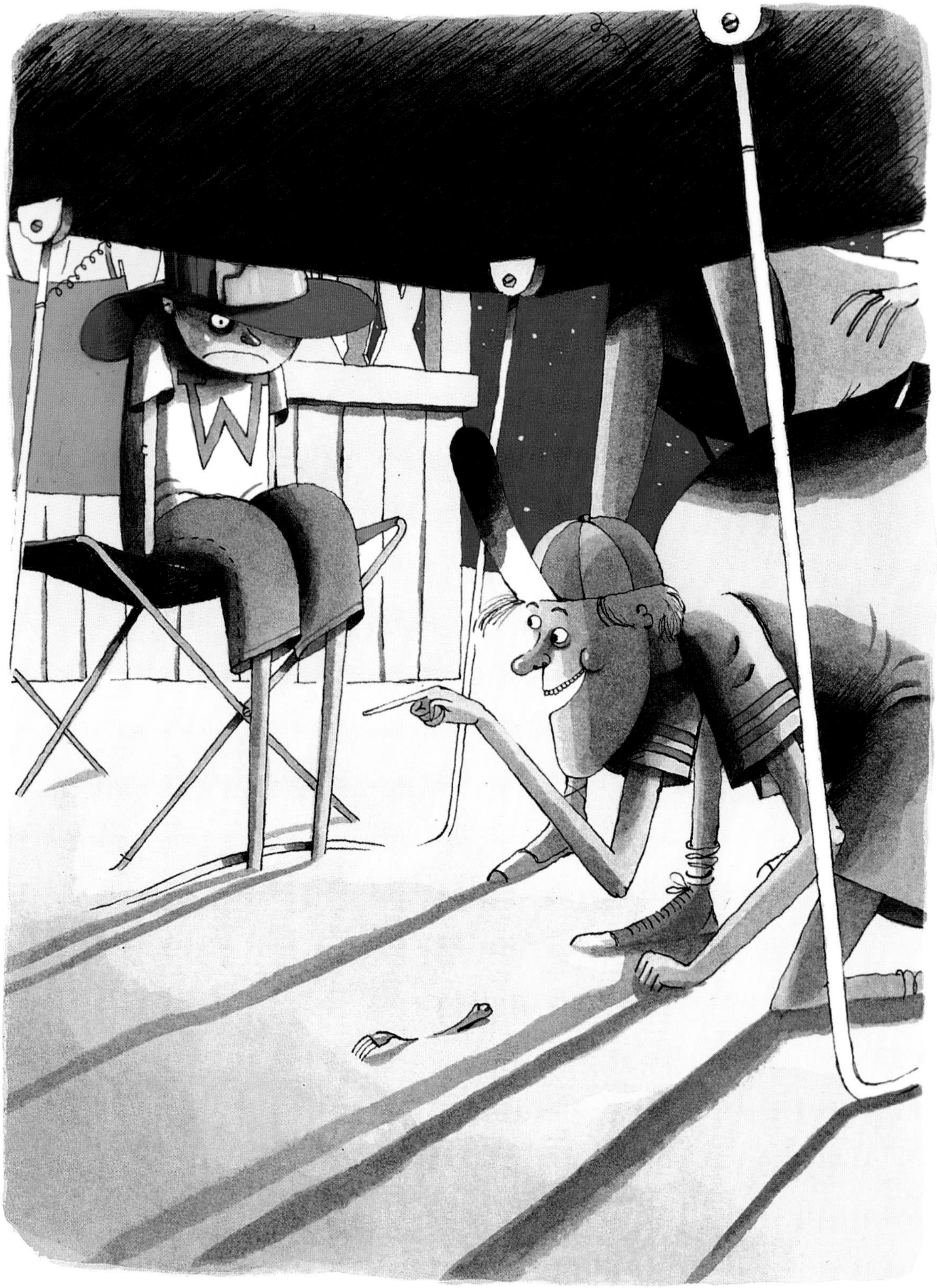

At suppertime Horace had a breakthrough. He saw that while Iris could swing her feet below the picnic bench, Wallace's bare feet were resting on the surface of the sand. Desperate to get a better look at Wallace's legs and feet, Horace picked up his arm, and with a single sharp swipe he knocked his milk into his plate and his fork under the table.

"Horace!" said his mother.

"What a slob," said Iris.

"Clean it up," said his father.

Now's my chance, thought Horace. He ducked under the table.

Wallace's feet had disappeared into the sand!

"Eureka!" yelled Horace, and banged his head on the underside of the table. Rubbing the bruise with one hand, he crawled out, stood up, and pointed dramatically at Wallace. "Wallace," he said, staring at his brother, "is growing down."

"What?" said Iris, his mother, and his father, all at once.

"Wallace," Horace said, "is not growing up. He is growing down."

"Stand up, Wallace!" said his mother.

Wallace stood up. It was true. Anybody really looking at Wallace could see immediately that his legs were very long. He looked like a kite at the end of a string.

Wallace's mother whipped out her tape measure.

"Wallace's legs," she announced, "have grown six inches since last Tuesday!" She hit her head with the palm of her hand. "Oh, what shall I do, what shall I do?"

Wallace sat at the table. He felt that his destiny had been taken out of his hands. It was an odd feeling, but he was a child and it was not entirely new to him. He saw how tall his mother looked in the light from the porch. Would he grow taller than the roof? Than the trees?

Suddenly Wallace's mother was gone. There was the sound of an engine, and as they ran to the porch, they could see the car racing down the hill with their mother at the wheel, heading into the night.

Where was she going?

Wallace's mother drove over dark roads, over spidery bridges, on highways thick with cars, beside a glinting river. She was on her way to see Nanny Heppleweather.

Nanny Heppleweather was very, very old. When Horace, and then Wallace, and then Iris, was born, Mrs. Hoskins had begged Nanny Heppleweather to come, but she had refused.

"I'm too old, my dear," Nanny Heppleweather had said. "But if you ever need any real help—real help, mind you, not the ordinary kind—you come straight to me, and I'll see what I can do.

"Come in," said Nanny Heppleweather, when, tired and thirsty and hours after she had started out, Wallace's mother knocked at the door.

Nanny Heppleweather was sitting in a huge velvet chair with a cat in her lap. "You have come at last, my dear. It's that second boy of yours, isn't it. Wallace."

"Yes," said Wallace's mother. "You see, Nanny, Wallace... well, you know up until now he's been quite small, but—"

"Shhh," said Nanny Heppleweather. Then she said something so softly that Wallace's mother had to bend down and put her ear very close to the old woman's mouth.

"What?" said Wallace's mother.

"Does he wear a hat?" whispered Nanny Heppleweather. Wallace's mother nodded.

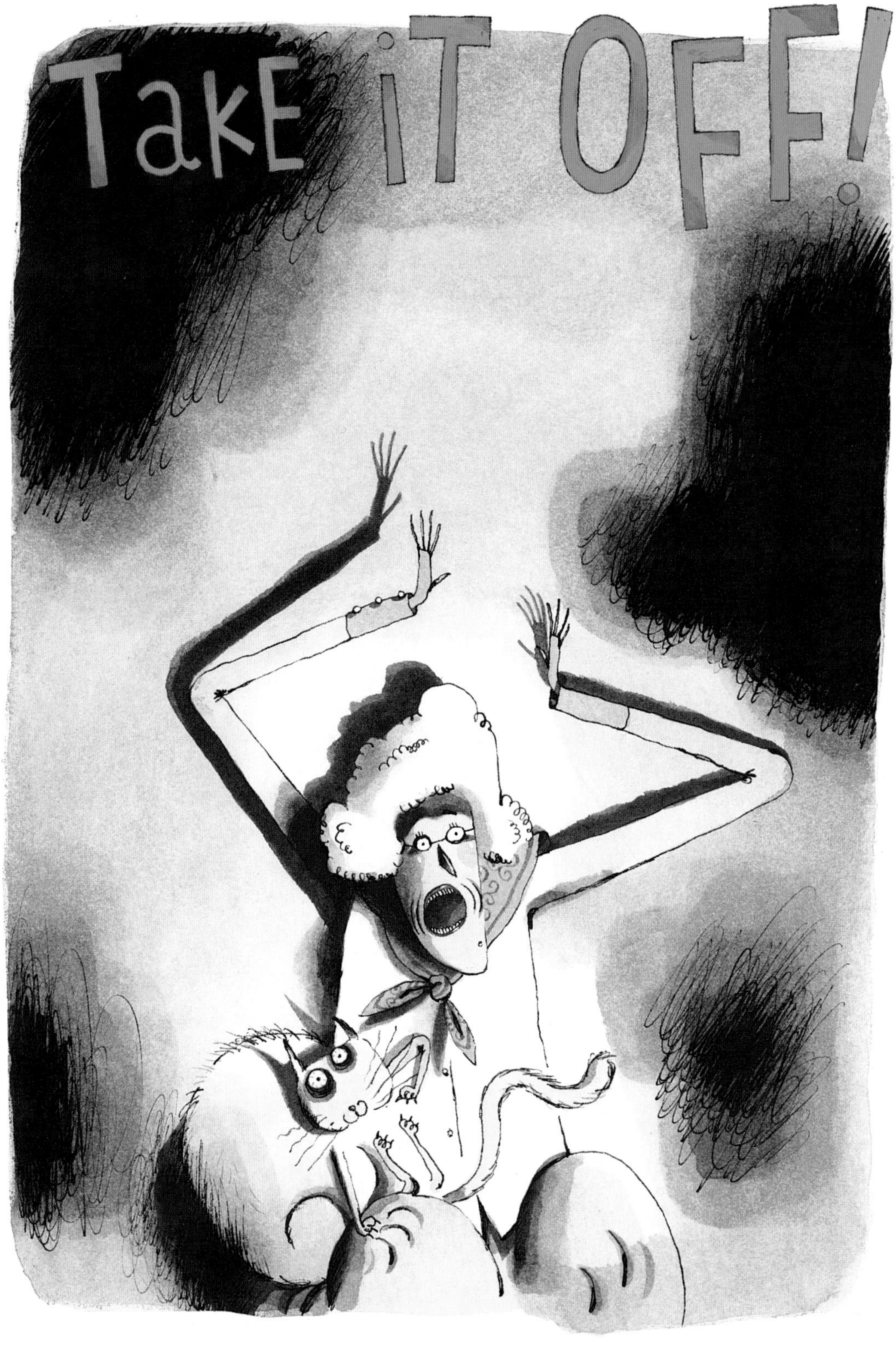
TakE iT OFF!

yelled Nanny Heppleweather, so loudly that Wallace's mother jumped back. "Take off the hat," she repeated. "When you do, you will find a toadstool growing on the boy's head. Pick it and cut it into ten pieces. Take these and throw them into the sea. Take the hat and put it where the boy can see it. He will no longer want it, but he will like to know where it is. Then go to bed."

"But what—" said Wallace's mother. But Nanny had fallen asleep.

Mrs. Hoskins closed the door quietly. Full of unanswered questions, she drove past the still dark hills, over the bridges, and past the quiet fields.

Upstairs at the cottage, Wallace's legs, shooting out of his pajama bottoms, seemed to grow as she watched. Gently she took off his fireman's hat. She jumped as a tiny toad, no bigger than a baby's thumb, hopped out.

Under a tangle of hair, glowing in the dark, was an orange toadstool.

She picked it.

Then she hung Wallace's hat on the bedpost, took the toadstool downstairs, and cut it carefully into ten pieces.

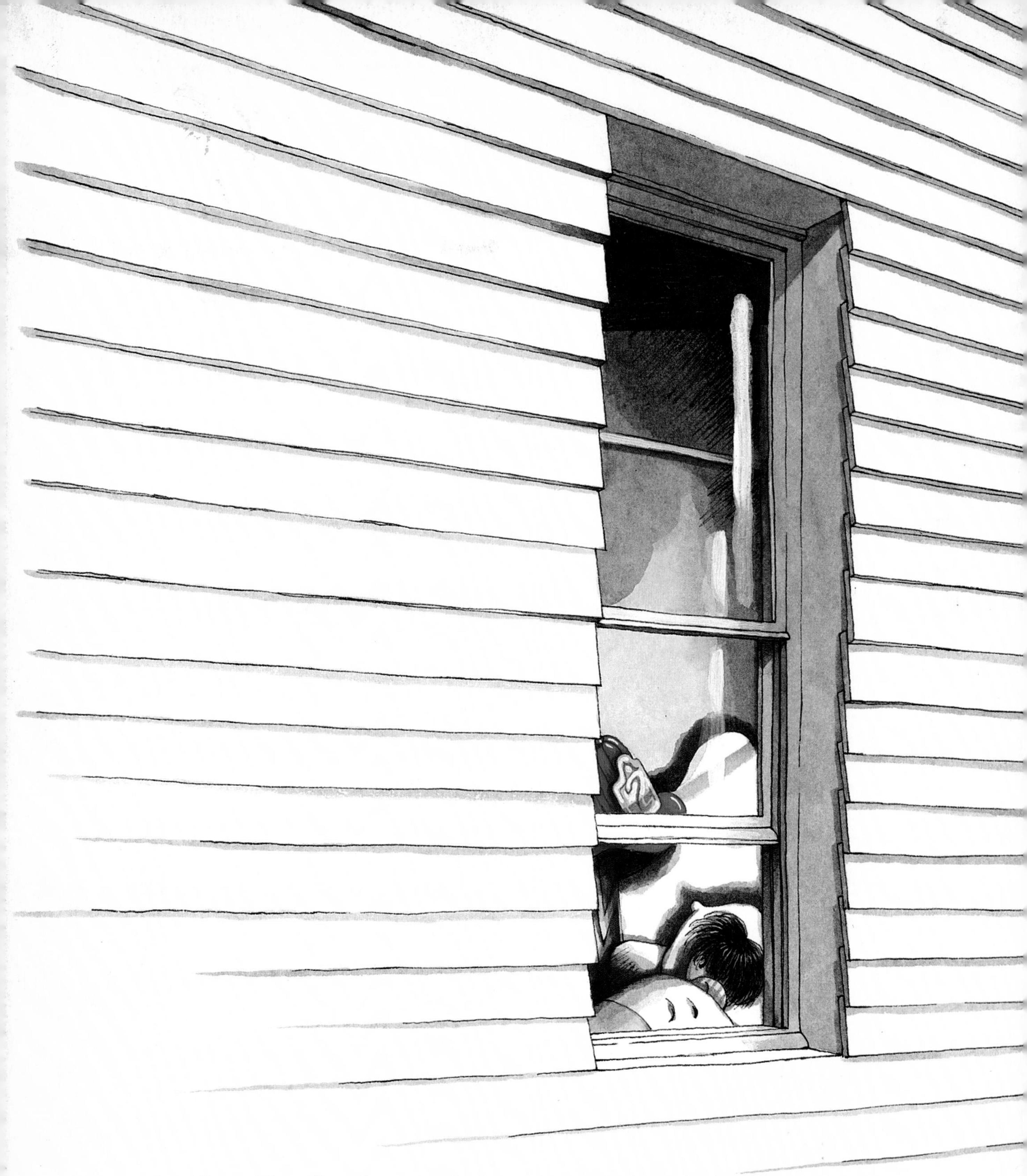

Outside, the sky was looped with garlands of stars. Wallace's mother walked down to the beach and threw the pieces of toadstool into the waves. Did they seem to flutter on the water? They hissed in the surf, and were gone.

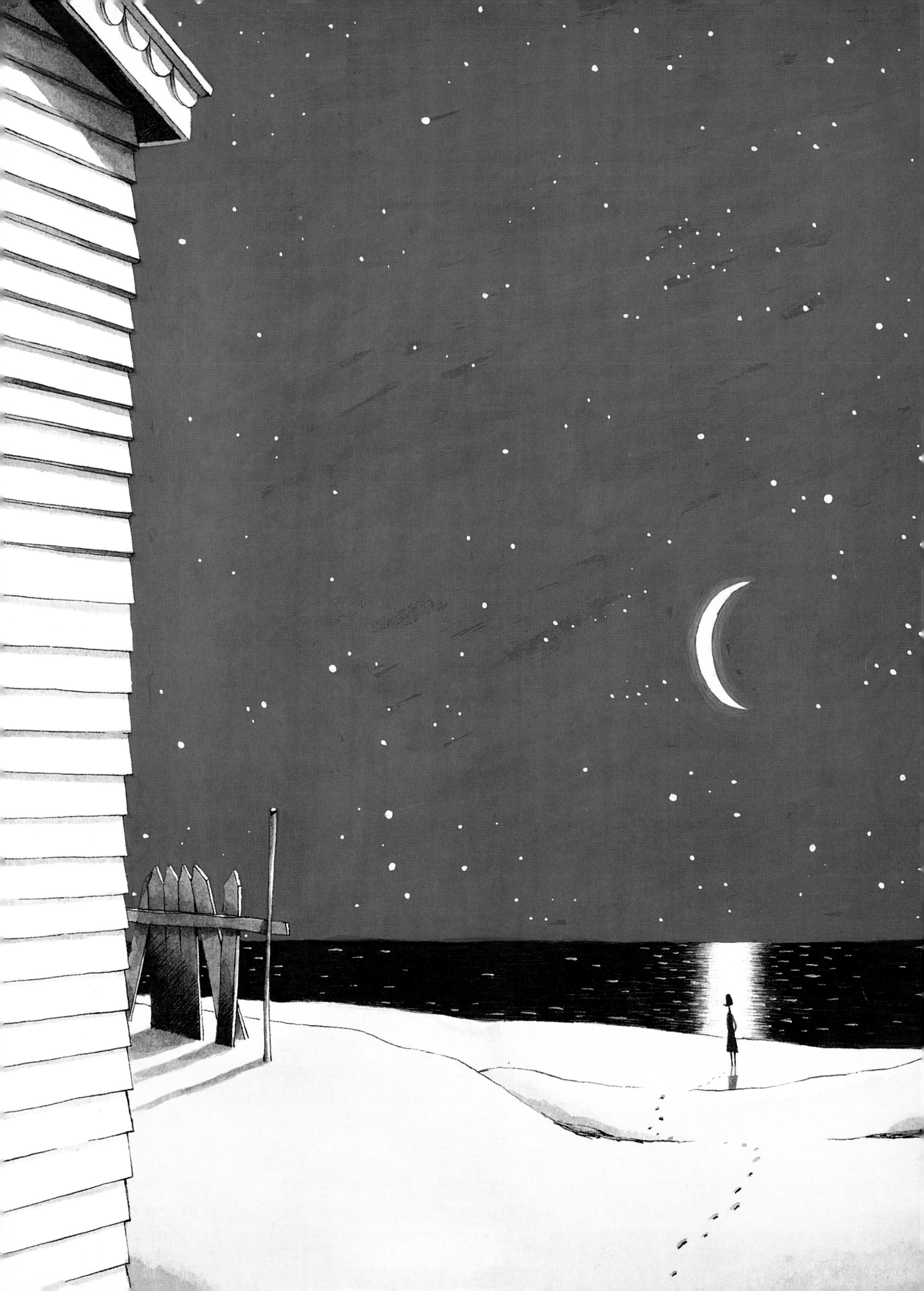

The next morning Wallace was the last to come down to breakfast. His head was bare. His pajama legs stopped at his knees. The seams of his pajama top had split, and the buttons had popped. When he sat down at the table he was taller than Iris but smaller than Horace. He was exactly in the middle.

"Boy needs a haircut," said Wallace's father.

Iris and Horace looked as if they were going to begin talking at once. Wallace's mother raised a finger to her lips.

"But—" said Horace.

Wallace's mother shook her head. She smiled at Wallace's father. "Well, Fergus," she said, "you were right. He did grow out of it."

Wallace looked at his mother. Then he stretched. He stretched from the tips of his fingers to the end of his toes. It felt to him as though something had happened, something mysterious and strange. He reached up and scratched the top of his head.

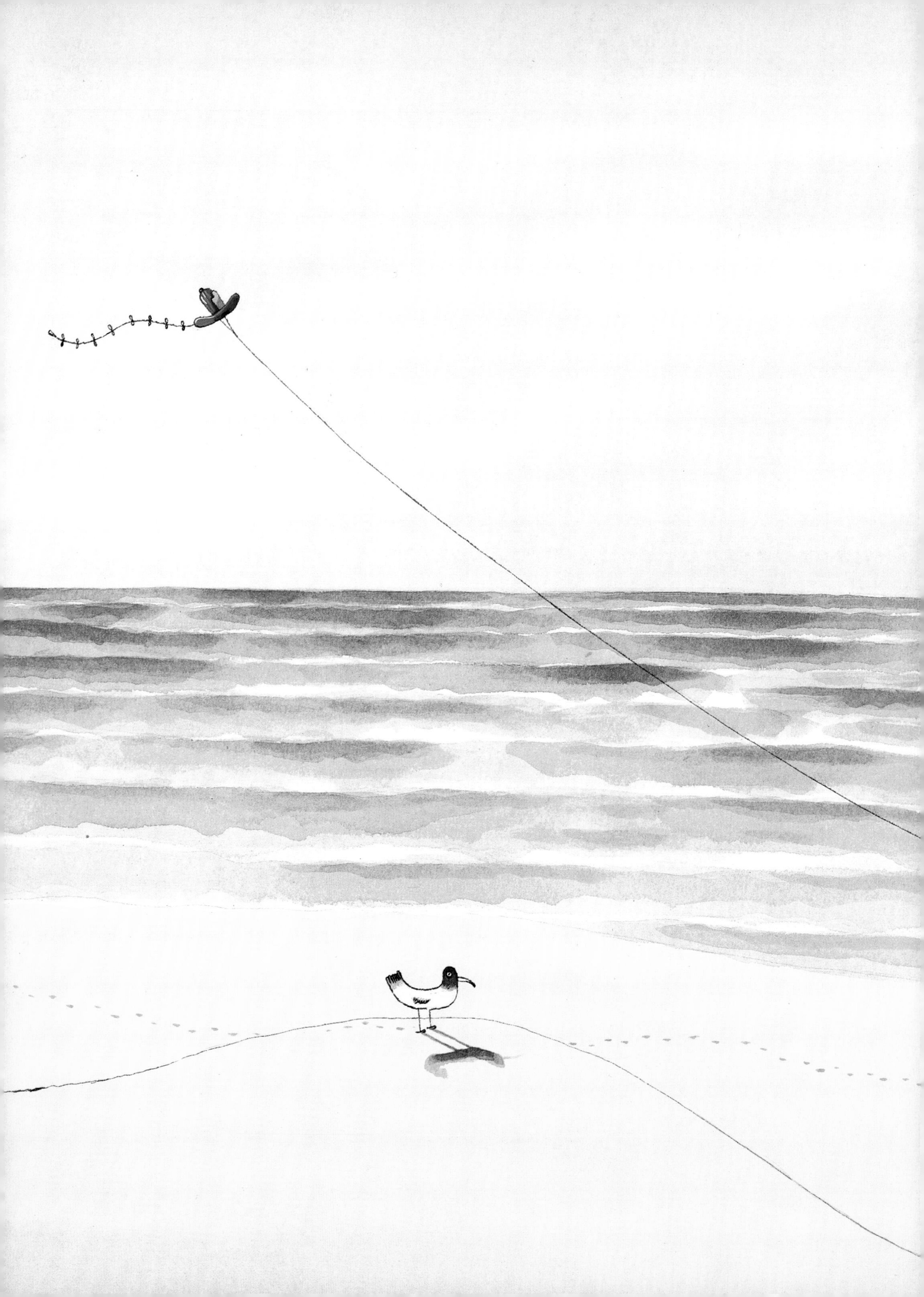

For the first time in days, he grinned. Then he applied himself to his breakfast. He had lost his appetite during his long days of private worry, and now he was starving. When he was done, he took a deep breath.

Outside, the morning was full of pale sunshine, and a few clouds were drifting like islands along the shiny horizon. He would think it all over later. For now, there was a brisk wind. There was plenty to do.

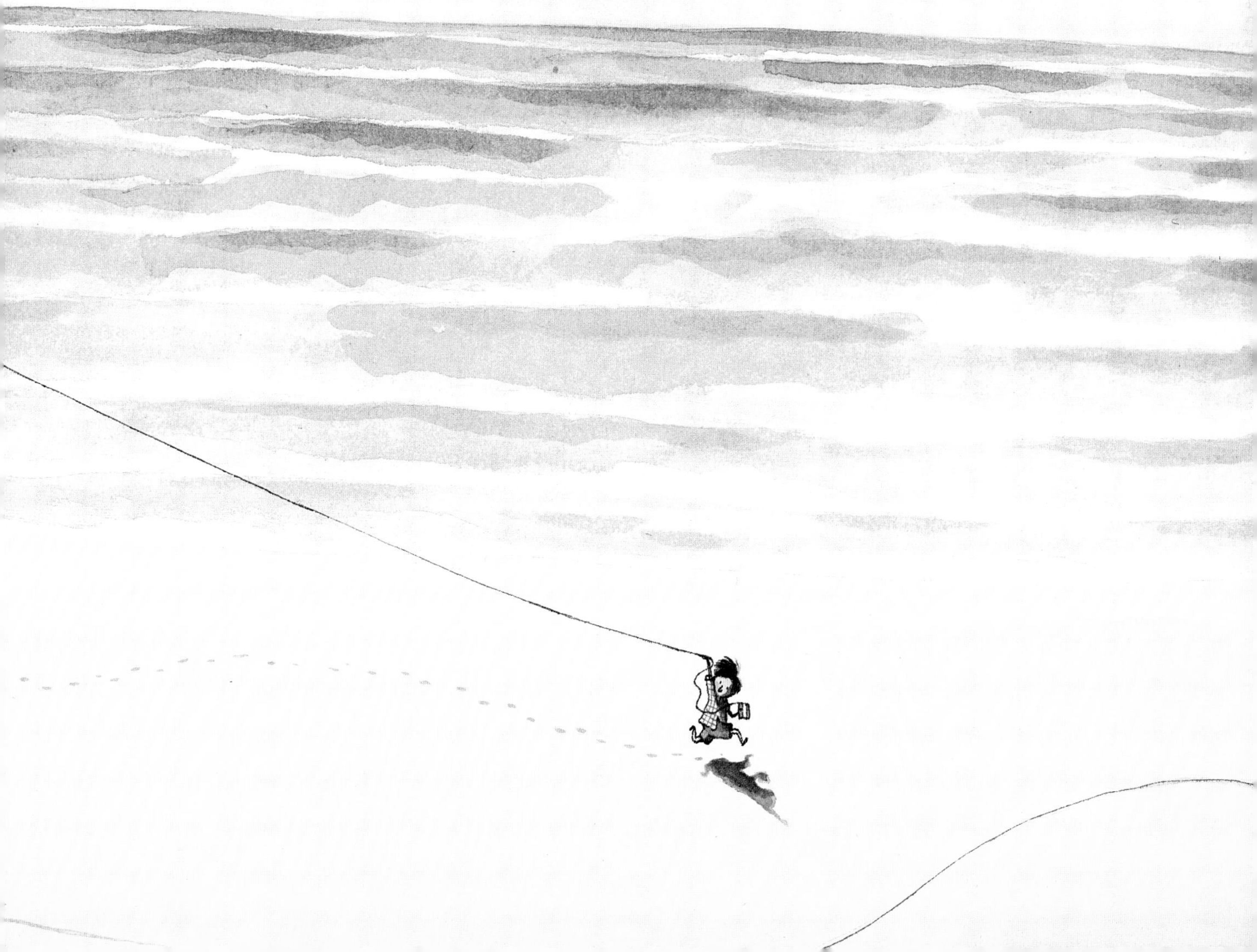